MEET THE THUNDERBIRDS

Adapted by Namrata Tripathi

Illustrated by Aristides Ruiz and Mike Giles

Based on a motion picture screenplay by
William Osborne and Michael McCullers

Story by Peter Hewitt and William Osborne

Based on the original television series
"Thunderbirds" © ITC Distribution, LLC

HarperFestival®
*A Division of HarperCollins*Publishers

Meet the Tracy family:
Jeff, John, Scott,
Virgil, Gordon, and Alan.

They are the members of a secret
group called International Rescue.
The International Rescue team
travels all over the world helping
people in need.

They use special rescue vehicles
on their missions.
These machines are called *Thunderbirds*.

Because their vehicles are so famous, people call the International Rescue team the Thunderbirds, too.

Space Agency, Jeff counts himself amongst the
sation.
Entrepreneurial, spirited and adventurous, Jeff
g made him one of the richest men in the world,

Intelligent
kindly an
ation der
Jeff is a
and ra
allows
astro
him
whe
sel

v
i

This is Jeff Tracy.
He started International Rescue.
He runs the Thunderbird command
station on Tracy Island.

Jeff's friend Brains helps him.
From Tracy Island, they can keep track
of what all the Thunderbirds are doing.

Jeff's sons Virgil, John, Scott, and Gordon make up the rest of the Thunderbirds team.

Scott works with
Thunderbird 1.
It is a shiny silver rocket
ship with a red nose cone.

It is always first on the scene in an emergency.
Thunderbird 1 is so fast it can rocket up to 15,000 miles per hour.

Jeff or his son Gordon pilot *Thunderbird 2*.
Thunderbird 2 is a huge green airship.
It carries supplies to the other Thunderbirds.
It also carries *Thunderbird 4*, a submarine.

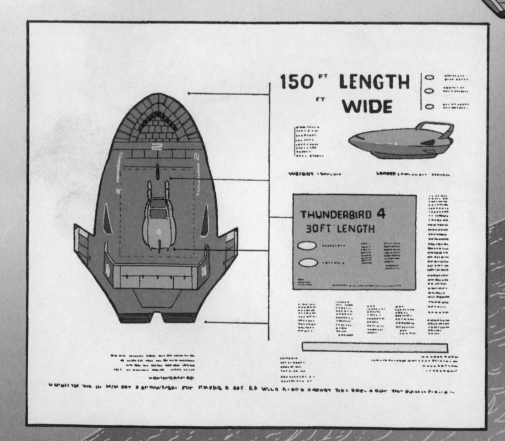

Thunderbird 2 is the busiest of the fleet.

Virgil pilots *Thunderbird 3*.
Thunderbird 3 is a space-rescue rocket.
When it is in space, *Thunderbird 3*
docks at *Thunderbird 5*.

Watch out for the flames and smoke
when *Thunderbird 3* takes off—
3 . . . 2 . . . 1 . . . . Blast off!

Thunderbird 4 is a yellow submarine.
It can dive deep into the ocean
for underwater rescue missions.

John is the oldest of the Tracy boys.
He works on *Thunderbird 5*.
Thunderbird 5 is a space station.
John's job is out of this world!

From up here, John can keep an eye
on what is going on all over the planet.
He can send important data to the rest
of the International Rescue team.

Meet Alan—the youngest Tracy.
He wishes he could join his brothers
on their missions.
But Alan has to finish school first.

Fermat is Alan's best friend.

He is Brains' son.

He tries to keep Alan out of trouble.

Sometimes it is Alan who needs
to be rescued.
Like when he gets into trouble with
the headmaster.
That's where Lady Penelope comes in.

Lady Penelope is a beautiful secret agent.
She often lends the Thunderbirds a hand.
(But she is careful never to break a nail!)

Lady Penelope rides around in *FAB 1*, her pink limousine.

When Lady Penelope needs to get somewhere fast, *FAB 1* becomes an airplane.

Parker is Lady Penelope's right-hand man.
He makes sure no one gives her trouble.

Bad guys, watch out. . . .
Here come the Thunderbirds!